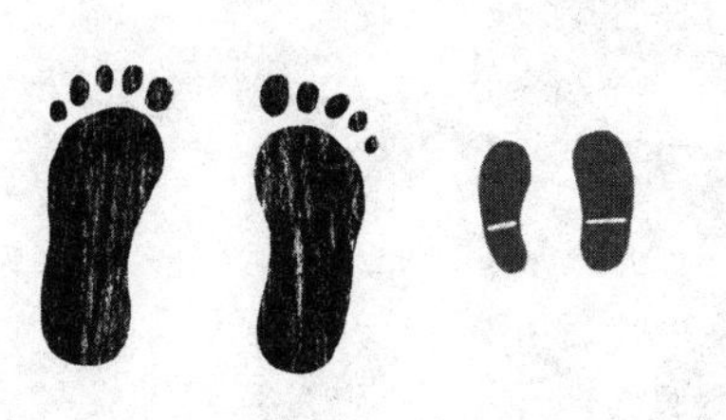

BIGFOOT and LITTLE FOOT

BOOK 3

THE SQUATCHICORNS

Story by Ellen Potter

Art by Felicita Sala

AMULET BOOKS

NEW YORK

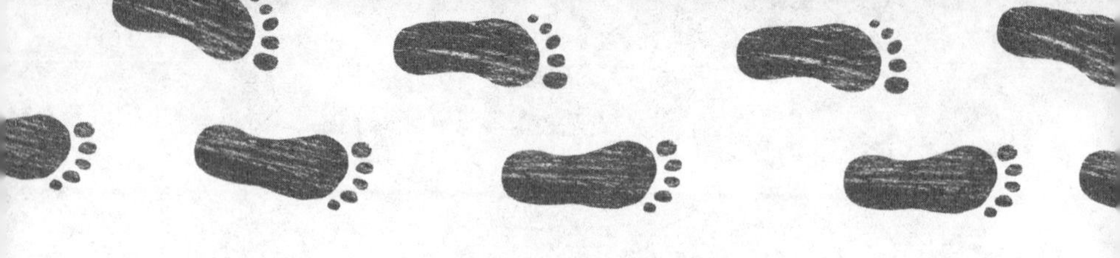

For Amelia Socorro Boscana,
who is her very own superhero

PUBLISHER'S NOTE: This is a work of fiction. Names, characters, places, and incidents are either the product of the author's imagination or used fictitiously, and any resemblance to actual persons, living or dead, business establishments, events, or locales is entirely coincidental.

Library of Congress Cataloging-in-Publication Data

Names: Potter, Ellen, 1963- author. | Sala, Felicita, illustrator.
Title: The Squatchicorns / by Ellen Potter; illustrated by Felicita Sala.
Description: New York: Amulet Books, 2019. | Series: Big Foot and Little Foot ; book 3 | Summary: A tribe of odd-looking Sasquatches flee their cursed cave and take refuge with Hugo, but when Hugo invites Nobb, one of the strange squidges to Boone's birthday party, the result is near-disaster. Identifiers: LCCN 2018028186 (print) | LCCN 2018034679 (ebook) | ISBN 9781683354789 (ebooks) | ISBN 9781419733642 (hardcover) Subjects: | CYAC: Sasquatch–Fiction. | Friendship–Fiction. | Blessing and cursing–Fiction. | Birthdays–Fiction. | Parties–Fiction.
Classification: LCC PZ7.P8518 (ebook) | LCC PZ7.P8518 Sq 2019 (print) | DDC [E]–dc23

Book design by Siobhán Gallagher

Printed and bound in U.S.A.
10 9 8 7 6 5 4 3 2 1

ABRAMS The Art of Books
195 Broadway, New York, NY 10007
abramsbooks.com

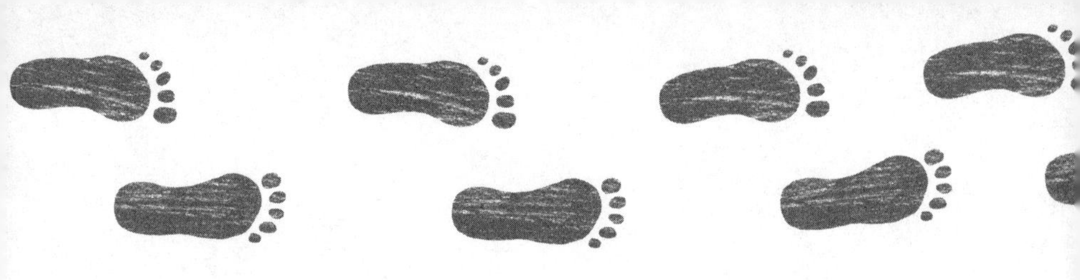

The Big Foot and Little Foot series

Book One: *Big Foot and Little Foot*

Book Two: *The Monster Detector*

Book Three: *The Squatchicorns*

1

Castles & Knights

Deep in the cold North Woods there lived a young Sasquatch named Hugo. He was bigger than you but smaller than me, and he was hairier than both of us. He lived in apartment 1G in the very back of Widdershins Cavern with his mother and father and his older sister, Winnie.

It was Saturday morning, and Hugo and his friend Gigi were sitting on the floor playing a game they had made up called Castles & Knights. They used cups turned upside down for the castles. For the roads, they used sticks, and they had painted faces on rocks for their characters. There

were smooth bits of red and green and blue glass that Hugo's grandpa had found in the woods while hunting mushrooms—these were the magic gems.

"My knight is crossing the moat to attack your castle," Gigi said, pushing a painted rock forward.

"Okay, then my wizard is going to open the secret trapdoor," Hugo said, "and a Snallygaster is going to fly out and attack your knight."

Gigi looked at Hugo.

"A Snallygaster? You can't make up creatures out of your head, Hugo. Maybe you could use a dragon. Or a Minotaur."

"But there really is such a thing as a Snallygaster! Hold on, I'll prove it."

Hugo got up and walked over to his bookshelf.

Rick-a-tick-a-tick.

Gigi frowned at the sound.

From the bookshelf, Hugo pulled out a very thick hardcover book called *The Biggest Ever Book of Cryptids*. His best friend, Boone, had lent the book to him, and Hugo had been reading it every day. Even when it was past his bedtime, he would read the book under his blankets, using his jar of glowworms for light. The book listed all the known cryptids (which is a fancy word for "mysterious creatures") in alphabetical order. It had full-color illustrations of each one of them, too. Once in a while, there was a photograph of a cryptid, but those

were usually pretty blurry and could just as easily have been something else.

Hugo walked back to Gigi to show her the book.

Rick-a-tick-a-tick.

"Hugo," Gigi said, staring down at Hugo's feet, "when was the last time you cut your toenails?"

"I don't know. Why?" Hugo sat down beside her and leafed through the book to find the section about Snallygasters.

"Because your toenails are so long that they're clicking against the ground."

Hugo ignored this. He flipped through

the pages, past pictures of creatures that he had never heard of before reading the book. There was an Owlman and Swamp Monsters and Tommyknockers and Globsters. Some of the creatures were no bigger than a pinkie toe, and others were taller than the tallest pine tree.

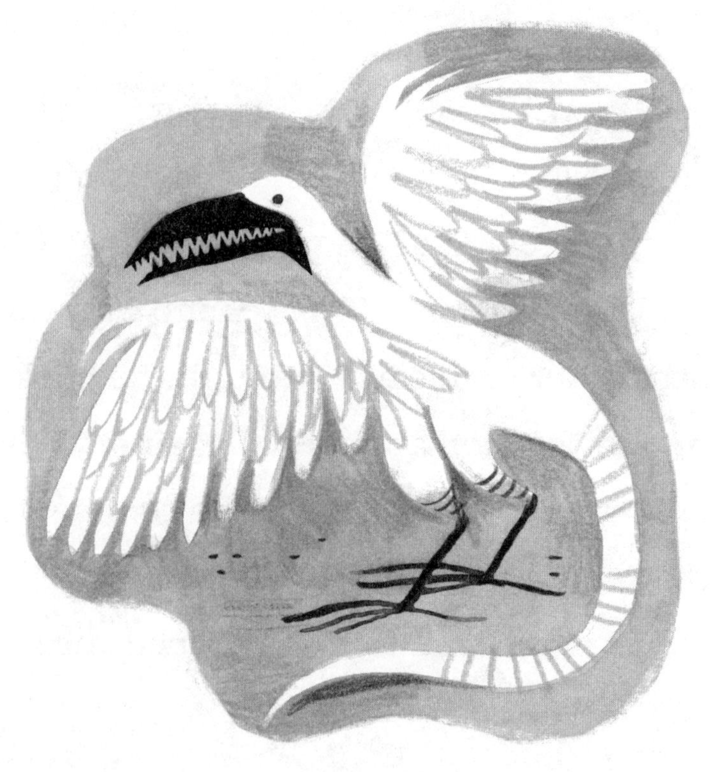

"Snallygaster! Here it is!" Hugo pointed at a page with a picture of a snaky-looking beast. He read, "'A dragon-like creature that is half bird, half reptile, with razor-sharp teeth.' There! I told you they were a real thing!"

Right then they heard the noise again.

Rick-a-tick-a-tick.

"Well, that's obviously not my toe-nails," Hugo told Gigi.

Hugo stood up and walked over to the little stream that ran right through his bedroom. It entered the room through a hole in the bottom of the wall, then it wiggled across the room and exited through another hole in the wall by Hugo's toy chest. The little stream was

Hugo's personal floating post office, since that's how he and Boone sent messages to each other.

Rick-a-tick-a-tick.

A wooden toy boat sailed through the hole in the wall and into Hugo's room. A little bottle was *rick-a-tick-a-tick*ing around inside the boat. And in that bottle was a note from Boone.

2

The Absolute Most Perfect Present

Hugo unscrewed the bottle's lid and took out the rolled-up note, which was tied with a thin green ribbon.

"Hmm, this looks fancier than usual," Hugo said as he untied the ribbon and rolled out the note. It said:

Dear Hugo,

You are cordially invited to Boone's birthday party. (Don't worry, there won't be any other Humans there besides me and Grandma!)

Place: Boone's House

Day: Today

Time: Noon, just in time for lunch and birthday cake

Boone

Hugo looked up at Gigi. "A Human birthday party!" he exclaimed. "Do you think it will be different from a Sasquatch birthday party?"

Gigi considered. "Well, I would guess that they don't pull out three hairs from your chin for good luck," she said.

"Probably not. Boone doesn't have any hair on his chin," Hugo said. "But do you think he'll get to be King for a Day?"

When a young Sasquatch has a birthday, he or she wears a Birthday Crown, which makes them King or Queen for a Day. That means they can do whatever they want to do for the whole day.

"I've read lots of books about Humans, but I've never read about Humans having Birthday Crowns," Gigi said.

“That’s too bad. Being King for a Day is the best part of a birthday.”

“I do think Humans get presents, though, like we do,” Gigi said.

“Oh.” Hugo thought. “I wonder what present I should give him.”

“You could make him a little book of word puzzles,” Gigi suggested. “Like the one I made for you on your last birthday.”

“I *could* do that . . .” Hugo pretended to think about this, but that book of puzzles was now in a box at the bottom of his closet. “Hmm, maybe he’d rather have something else instead.”

“Well, what does he like?” Gigi asked.

“He likes cryptids.”

“You can’t give him a cryptid,” Gigi said.

"No," Hugo agreed. He looked around his room for other ideas and spotted a clickity-clack under his bed.

In case you don't know, a clickity-clack is a piece of string with a walnut on either end. Holes are made in each walnut for the string to go through. You pick up the string in the middle and bob it up and down to make the walnuts clack against each other.

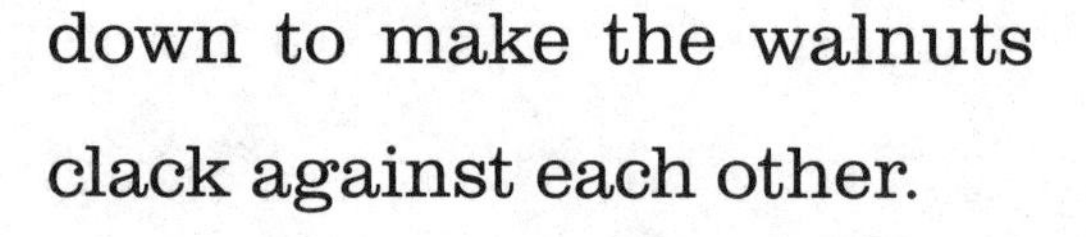

"Maybe I could make him a clickity-clack," Hugo said.

"Too noisy." Gigi winced.

Hugo thought some more.

"Wait! I know what I'll give him!" he cried out.

"And it's definitely something he doesn't already have!"

When he told Gigi what it was, she had to admit that it *was* a good present, even if it wasn't a book of word puzzles. Hugo spent the next hour making Boone's birthday gift, with Gigi's help. When they finished, they both agreed it was the absolute most perfect present for Boone. They had just begun to wrap it when the door swung open and Hugo's sister, Winnie, burst in.

"QUICK! HIDE!" Winnie shrieked. "WIDDERSHINS CAVERN IS BEING INVADED!"

HUGO

3

The Invasion

Winnie made a mad dash for Hugo's closet and slammed the door shut.

Hugo and Gigi looked at each other.

Hugo shrugged.

Gigi shrugged back.

They both knew that Winnie was very dramatic.

“By the way, who’s invading us?” Hugo called to Winnie.

“An army of Sasquatches with unicorn horns on their heads!” Winnie called back.

“Do they have sparkly rainbow tails, too?” Hugo asked.

Gigi giggled.

“Ha, ha, ha!” Winnie shouted angrily. “You two better come in here and hide if you know what’s good for you.”

“We’re fine out here, thanks,” Hugo said. “Anyway, we’ve never seen a Sasquatch unicorn before.”

“A Squatchicorn,” Gigi suggested.

And of course that made them laugh even harder. Winnie popped her head out of the closet and glared at them.

"Well, if you two don't believe me, why don't you just go outside and see for yourselves?" Then she shut herself back in the closet.

Hugo and Gigi looked at each other.

"Why not?" said Gigi.

They marched out of the bedroom, into the living room, and opened the front door.

Walking up the passageway outside Hugo's apartment were two Sasquatches whom Hugo and Gigi had never seen before. And sprouting out of each of their foreheads was an honest-to-goodness unicorn horn.

4

Squatchicorns

They're *real*!" Gigi whispered. "Squatchicorns!"

Hugo started to shut the door, and he would have locked it, too, but the bigger Squatchicorn rushed toward him, calling, "Wait! Are you Hugo?"

"Yes," said Hugo cautiously.

"And you must be Winnie?" the

Squatchicorn said to Gigi.

Gigi was too shocked to speak.

"That's Gigi," Hugo said. "Winnie's hiding."

From the other room, Winnie yelled out, "You get the award for biggest mouth, Hugo!"

"My name is Nogg," the Squatchicorn said. He held out his hand, and Hugo shook it. "This is my sister, Yama. Our parents are at your family's bakery right now. Your mom said we could wait for them here, in your apartment."

"Um . . . come in, I guess," Hugo said uncertainly.

As the two Squatchicorns walked into the apartment, Hugo spied another group of Squatchicorns walking by in the passageway outside. So it *was* an invasion! Only, they didn't seem like very scary invaders.

Nogg and Yama were both squidges, which is what you call a young Sasquatch.

Nogg was very tall and looked to be a few years older than Hugo, while his sister, Yama, was a few years younger than Hugo. Their hair was the usual Sasquatch sort of hair, and their bodies were Sasquatchy, too, but their horns were gray and stuck straight out of their foreheads.

They must be some sort of cryptid that Boone's book didn't know about, thought Hugo. Just like a Snallygaster was part bird, part reptile, Nogg and Yama were part Sasquatch, part unicorn.

"Would you like something to eat?" Gigi asked, nudging Hugo, because that was really what *he* should have asked.

"Sure," said Nogg.

He and his sister sat down while Hugo and Gigi went into the kitchen. Hugo opened up the cabinets and looked at the shelves. There were jars of acorn butter and pickled mushrooms and blackberry preserves. There was a wild sorrel–and–onion tart and a gooseberry pie and a bowl of hazelnuts.

"What do you think Squatchicorns eat?" he asked Gigi.

"Well, unicorns are sort of like horses," Gigi said, "and horses eat grass."

"I don't think we have grass," Hugo said, looking up at the cabinets.

Gigi thought for a moment.

"What about pillows? They're stuffed with straw."

"Good thinking!"

First they went to Hugo's room to get his pillow. But then he remembered that Winnie's pillow was fatter than his, so they went to Winnie's room and took her pillow to the kitchen. Carefully, Hugo pulled apart the stitches. Then he reached inside the pillow, took out handfuls of straw, and divided it up between two plates.

Hugo and Gigi looked at the plates of straw doubtfully.

"I wish it looked more delicious," he said.

"It may not look delicious to us, but it will probably look delicious to a Squatchicorn," Gigi said.

Hugo guessed so. But just in case, he

put a few hazelnuts on top of each pile of straw for decoration.

It would be nice to have a horn on your head, Hugo thought, but he couldn't imagine life without an acorn butter-and-raspberry cream sandwich every now and then.

5

Nogg and Yama

Nogg looked at his plate of straw with a strange expression on his face. Hugo worried that he could tell it came from a pillow, so he said, "We usually have better straw. I don't think it's in season now."

"I'm sure it's fine," Nogg said. But he picked up a hazelnut and nibbled on that instead.

Maybe Squatchicorns don't eat hay after all, thought Hugo.

Yama, however, didn't even eat the hazelnuts. She just sat on the floor beside her brother, looking very glum.

"She's upset that we had to leave our cavern," Nogg explained. "Our whole clan left yesterday. We all slept in the woods last night."

Hugo knew that sometimes Sasquatches had to abandon their caverns. Usually it was because a Human had found out where they lived, so it wasn't safe to stay there anymore.

Hugo couldn't imagine ever leaving Widdershins Cavern. He loved his room with its little stream running through

it. He loved helping his grandpa make snarfles on Sunday mornings at the Everything-You-Need General Store and Bakery. He even loved his school. It would be awful to have to leave all that behind. And what if he had to move to a cavern far, far away from the North Woods and Ripple Worm River? What if he had to move far, far away from Boone?

That would be the worst part.

"All my things are back in Craggy Cavern," Yama said miserably. "All my stuffed animals, all my drawings."

"You'll make new drawings," her brother told her.

"They won't be as good!" she insisted. "*And* I had to leave the fairy house I made in school, which was the biggest, most beautifulest one I ever made."

"Why didn't you take them with you?" asked Gigi.

"There was no time to pack." Yama's eyes grew wide and frightened. "We had to leave right away because of the–" But before she could say anything else, Nogg gave her a sharp, warning nudge with his elbow.

"*Shh*, you'll scare them," Nogg said under his breath.

Hugo and Gigi exchanged looks.

One thing was clear–the Squatchicorns had a secret.

6

The Big Wide World

Hugo's parents came home looking tired, but happy.

"Everyone pitched in to find extra dens in Widdershins Cavern, so your clan will all have places to sleep until you can find your new home," Dad told Nogg and Yama.

"Thank you," they said.

"You and your family are staying just down the passageway," Hugo's mom told them. "And you can come to our bakery for lunch."

"Lunch!" Hugo cried, suddenly remembering. "Boone invited me to his house for his birthday party today. I was thinking that Grandpa could take me there."

"Oh, Hugo, I'm sorry, but Grandpa will be much too busy at the bakery with all our new guests," his mom said. "So will your dad and I."

"Then I'll go on my own," Hugo declared.

"Absolutely not," his father said. "Young squidges cannot go tromping through the woods on their own."

"But it's Boone's birthday! I *have* to go!"

"I can take him," Nogg offered.

Hugo's mom and dad looked at Nogg, then glanced at each other, uncertain.

"I'm one merit badge away from being a Falcon in the Ranger Scouts, ma'am," said Nogg, "and I've hiked all over the North Woods by myself. I know every bit of it."

An hour later, Hugo, Nogg, and Hugo's mom stood by the mouth of Widdershins Cavern.

They were all holding something:

Hugo was holding Boone's present.

Nogg was holding a backpack.

And Hugo's mom was holding her tongue.

She wanted to say, “Don’t go! This is too dangerous!”

But she didn’t.

She knew how much Hugo wanted to make this trip to Boone’s house for his birthday.

“Do you have the Human Repellant spray?” she asked them.

Nogg felt around in the backpack that Hugo's dad had given him and pulled out the bright red can of Human Repellant. When you sprayed it, it made everything around you stink like skunk. When Sasquatches were walking through the woods, they usually took a can or two with them to keep the Humans away.

"And the glowworm lamp? And a fire-starting kit? And the compass?"

Nogg checked the backpack. "All here," he said.

"Okay." She took a deep breath. "Well, have a good time."

"We will," Hugo said.

"And remember to walk heel to toe."

That was the quietest way to walk in the woods.

"We will," Nogg promised her.

"Don't forget, anything can happen in the Big Wide World," she reminded them.

Hugo looked excited at the thought.

"And I don't mean good anythings!" Hugo's mother told him sternly.

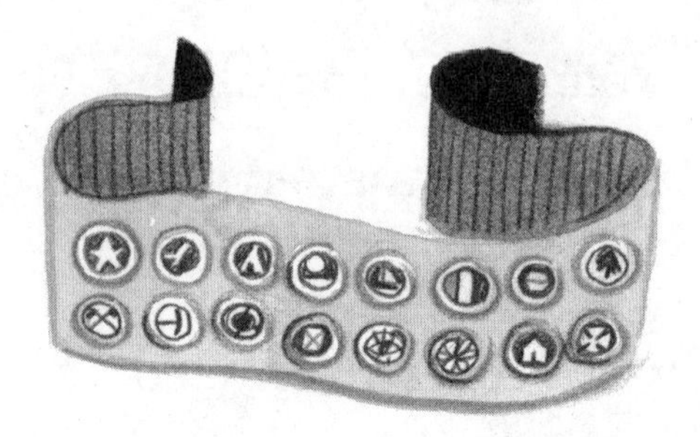

7

Nogg's Secret

It was a long walk to Boone's house. Every so often, Nogg stopped to sniff the air, making sure that no Humans were around.

They crossed Ripple Worm River by leaping from rock to rock where the river ran shallow. Mostly, though, they kept to the thickest part of the woods, walking without making a sound, as only Sasquatches can. Once, they even snuck up on a deer and her fawn as the pair were nibbling on buds from a tree. Hugo came so close to the deer that he reached out and petted the fawn's spotted back. The mother deer snorted in surprise but didn't run—animals know that Sasquatches won't hurt them.

"Nogg," Hugo said in his quietest voice when they were deep in the woods, "there's something I've been wondering about."

"What?" Nogg asked. He spoke in a voice so

quiet that if you heard it, you would have thought it was just the sound of leaves stirring in the wind.

"Why did your clan have to leave your cavern so quickly?"

"I don't think I should tell you," Nogg said. "You might get scared."

"Not me," Hugo said stoutly.

For a moment Nogg was silent. Then he whispered, "Do you believe in ghosts, Hugo?"

Hugo was not sure that he did believe in ghosts. But he was not sure that he didn't believe in them, either.

"I *might* believe in them," he said.

"Well, Craggy Cavern was haunted," Nogg said. "That's why we left."

"Haunted!" Hugo cried.

"Shhh."

"But how did you know it was haunted?" Hugo asked in a quieter voice.

"Well, about a month ago, our old cavern flooded, so we moved into Craggy Cavern. It was fine at first. But then strange things started happening. Stuff would go missing. My dad couldn't find his whittling knife, and Mrs. Wikpik's bracelet disappeared. My Ranger Scout sash with all my merit badges disappeared, too. If you were eating your lunch and walked away, your lunch would be gone when you came back."

"Rats?" suggested Hugo.

"That's what we thought at first. But

then things got stranger. We started seeing an eerie blue light floating through dark passages and then vanishing."

Hugo felt a shiver on his neck. "The ghost," he murmured.

Nogg nodded. "Then came the weird sounds. We would suddenly hear this knocking sound. And right after the knocking, something bad would happen. One time, a stalactite in the school lunchroom fell and almost hit someone. Another time, a loose rock fell from a ledge during recess and broke a teacher's foot."

That shivery feeling on Hugo's neck traveled down his back. He looked behind him, then all around. The woods suddenly felt very wild and sinister. He remembered

what his mother had said—that anything could happen in the Big Wide World . . . and not *good* anythings.

"Then yesterday," Nogg continued, "while we were sitting in class, we heard it again. *Knock, knock, knock*. Everyone got quiet. We knew something bad was about to happen. Even our teacher looked scared. Suddenly we heard a rumble, and

we all jumped out of our seats a second before the back wall caved in. A big chunk of rock landed right on my desk and smashed it to bits. If I hadn't jumped up in time . . ." Nogg shook his head grimly. "We left Craggy Cavern right then and there, before something even worse happened."

All of a sudden, Nogg stopped walking. Crouching down, he squinted suspiciously through the trees, sniffing at the air.

"What is it?" Hugo whispered hoarsely, feeling a rush of panic.

"Right there." Nogg pointed.

With his heart thumping in his chest, Hugo peered through the thick tangle of trees and brush. Nestled by the riverbank was a little blue house with a red roof.

They had arrived at Boone's place.

8

The Human House

Hugo stood in front of Boone's door without knocking. To be honest, he felt a little nervous. He had never been in a Human house before. He had definitely never been to a Human birthday party. He didn't know what to expect or how to act.

"Are you sure they're *friendly*

Humans?" Nogg asked, eyeing the house uneasily.

"Of course they are!" Hugo said. Seeing Nogg nervous made Hugo feel braver. He stepped up and knocked on the door.

In a moment, the door swung open and there was Boone, with his thirty-eight freckles and an extra-wide smile.

"You're here!" Boone cried, just as Grandma Ruthie stepped up behind him. Boone and his grandma noticed Nogg at the same time.

"Ohhh . . . hello," Boone said, staring with wide eyes at the horn on Nogg's forehead. Nogg was staring right back at Boone and his grandma. He had never seen a Human up close before, and had certainly never spoken with one.

"Well, we can't stand here all day gawking at each other, can we?" Grandma Ruthie said. "Come on inside. Lunch is ready. I hope you're both hungry."

"Sasquatches are always hungry!" Hugo declared. "Especially after walking through the woods."

But then he remembered that Nogg was only part Sasquatch, and he supposed unicorns might not get quite as hungry as Sasquatches.

“I mean, I guess we wouldn’t mind a bite or two of something,” Hugo added.

Hugo walked inside the Human house and gazed around. It was very bright inside, even brighter than it was outside. That was the first thing Hugo noticed. It was so bright that it made Hugo’s eyes water. It was not at all like being inside Widdershins Cavern, which was always nice and dim, like twilight. The walls in the Human house were all straight and smooth, unlike the bumpy cave walls. Hugo thought it might be nice to lick them, but he knew that wouldn’t be polite.

“Happy birthday, Boone,” Nogg said.

Hugo had been so amazed at the Human house that he had almost forgotten why

they were there. "Oh, yes, happy birthday, Boone!" He handed Boone his gift. "Gigi helped me make this."

"Thanks!" Boone untied the string and unwrapped the gift. Inside was a crown. It was made of branches woven together tightly, and it had bits of smooth colored glass glued to it. Hugo and Gigi had used the branches and the magic gems from Castles & Knights to make it.

"It's a Birthday Crown," Hugo explained. "When a squidge has a birthday, they get a crown to make them King or Queen for a Day. It means you get to tell everybody what to do the entire day."

"Awesome!" Boone put the crown on his head. It fit perfectly. He pointed a finger at his grandma and said, "I hereby command you . . ."

Grandma Ruthie raised an eyebrow at him.

"Just practicing," he told her with a grin.

There was a scuffling sound from down the hallway, and suddenly a large yellow Labrador appeared in the room.

Here is something you probably don't know about Sasquatches: They are scared of dogs. I mean, absolutely bonkers terrified. This is probably because Humans have used dogs to hunt Sasquatches for many hundreds of years, so you can't blame Sasquatches for being afraid.

At the sight of the dog, Nogg plastered himself against the wall, while Hugo lunged toward Boone and swept his friend

up in his arms to save him from the ferocious beast. Boone's crown toppled off his head, and the dog, whose name was Mogi, grabbed it up in his mouth and trotted out the open door.

"Don't tell me that two big fellows like you are afraid of a *dog*?" Grandma Ruthie said to Hugo and Nogg.

"Mogi won't hurt you," Boone said. "He's afraid of everything, even umbrellas."

"I'm sorry," Hugo said as he gently placed Boone back on his feet. "But what about your crown . . ."

By the time they found Mogi, he had turned Boone's Birthday Crown into a mangled, slobbery mess. The glass gems were gone, too.

"Oh, Boone," Hugo said miserably. This was a crummy start to a birthday party.

"It's okay." Boone patted Hugo on the back. "I'll just rinse off the spit."

Boone rinsed the crown, dried it off, and put it back on his head. All the branches had teeth marks on them, and they were sticking every which way. Boone looked like he had rolled around in a pile of branches.

"See," Boone said, "I can still wear it."

He could. Except he didn't look very kingly anymore.

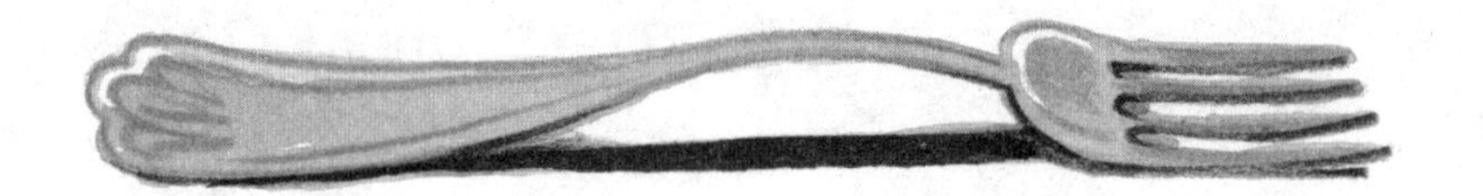

9
Slippery Strings

They all sat down in the dining room for lunch. The chairs were Human-sized, of course. That meant that Hugo and Nogg didn't quite fit in them. Although squidges are about the height of a small Human adult, they are a lot bulkier. They are all hair and thick arms and legs. Hugo was afraid he would break the chair, so he sort of squatted lightly on it.

The meal was strange—bowls of slippery white strings with a red sauce on top of them. Near each bowl was a metal stick with dangerous-looking spikes on it.

Hugo watched as Boone picked up the spikey metal stick, stabbed it into the slippery strings, and spun it around and around. Then with a *SLUUUURP*, he sucked the strings into his mouth.

Oh! Hugo realized. *The spikey metal thing is a Human spoon!*

Sasquatches don't have forks, only wooden spoons. And to be perfectly truthful, they often eat with their hands. Even when they have soup, they just drink it straight out of the bowl.

Hugo picked up the Human spoon. But it was so small in his large hand that he had a hard time twirling it in the strings the way Boone did. When he was finally able to get some of the strings into his mouth, he slurped it up like Boone had. *SLUUURP!* The red sauce splattered all over the hair on his chin and on his chest. He rubbed at it with his napkin, but that made it worse.

He looked over at Nogg. His face and chest were also a saucy mess.

Grandma Ruthie frowned at both of them. “Don’t tell me you two have never eaten spaghetti with tomato sauce.”

“Never,” Nogg said, rubbing at a splotch of sauce on his shoulder.

"I don't think I'm very good at spaghetti with tomato sauce," Hugo said.

"I can see that," she said.

"I'm *excellent* at birthday cake, though," Hugo assured her.

10

Human Birthday Cake

There was a chocolate cake on the kitchen counter. Hugo watched as Grandma Ruthie stuck little blue sticks in the cake. Then, to his surprise, she struck a match and lit those blue sticks.

"Boone!" Hugo whispered. "Why is she setting that cake on fire?"

“Those are birthday candles, Hugo,” Boone whispered back.

As Grandma Ruthie carried the cake with the lit candles over to the table, she sang the birthday song. You all know the song, but Hugo and Nogg didn’t, so they faked it as best they could, and by the time they had figured out the words, it ended.

Grandma Ruthie put the cake down in front of Boone and placed a different sort of Human spoon beside it. This one was shaped like a triangle with a long handle. It looked a lot less dangerous than the spaghetti spoon. Now, you and I both know that the triangle spoon was actually a cake server, but Sasquatches don’t have

such things, so of course Hugo wouldn't know that.

Boone closed his eyes. Then he just sat there like that, not moving or saying anything.

"Boone?" Hugo whispered.

Boone didn't answer.

"Boone? Are you sleeping?" Hugo was anxious to start eating the cake. He had barely eaten any of the spaghetti and after the long walk through the woods, his belly was feeling very empty and rumbly.

"I'm not sleeping, Hugo. I'm just thinking of a wish," Boone replied, his eyes still closed.

Hugo eyed the cake. "I can help you think of one," Hugo offered.

"I have to think of it myself," Boone told him.

Hugo sighed, but only in his head. While he waited for Boone to think of his wish, he picked up the triangle spoon to examine it.

"Okay, I know what I'll wish for!" Boone

said suddenly. He opened his eyes and blew out all the candles with one big breath.

After Boone plucked the candles out of the cake, he noticed that Hugo was holding the server. Boone slid the plate of cake toward Hugo.

"Go ahead," Boone said. "You can do the honors."

Hugo looked down at the beautiful cake.

"Are you sure?" he asked Boone.

"Why not?"

Hugo smiled. "Here goes," he said. He plunged the triangle spoon into the middle of the cake, scooped out a nice big chunk, and put it in his mouth.

The triangle spoon worked much better than the spaghetti spoon. In fact, it fit

his mouth so perfectly, he wondered why Sasquatches didn't have spoons like that, too.

When I get back home, he thought to himself, *I am going to mention this to Mom*.

Hugo took another spoonful of cake, and then another, all the while wishing that his cake was just a little bit bigger. Then he remembered his manners and stopped to wipe some frosting off his chin. That's when he noticed that no one else at the table had any cake in front of them. Not only that, but Boone and Grandma Ruthie were staring at him with shocked looks on their faces.

"Isn't anyone else going to have birthday cake?" Hugo asked them.

“Well, we were planning to,” Grandma Ruthie said in an annoyed voice.

Hugo looked over at the kitchen. He didn’t see any other cakes there. Then he looked down at his own cake.

“Is this . . . ?” he asked in a small, horrified voice.

“Yes, that’s the birthday cake,” Grandma Ruthie said. “The *only* birthday cake.”

“But it was so small that I just thought . . .” Hugo said.

Sasquatches have tremendous appetites, especially when it comes to cake. On their birthdays, everyone gets their very own cake. It would never have occurred to

Hugo that the puny little Human birthday cake was supposed to be shared.

"It's fine, Hugo," Boone said, though Hugo could tell that he was disappointed.

"It's not fine. I ate your birthday cake!" Hugo's eyes were welling up.

Grandma Ruthie couldn't stay irritated for long and said, "Now, now, we can't have tears at a birthday party. Never mind, it's just cake, and cake is a silly thing to cry about."

That was when Boone made his first command as King for a Day.

"I hereby declare that we go up to my tree house!"

So that's exactly what they did.

11
King Boone

Boone's tree house was made with nice strong planks of oak. It had windows cut into it and a rope ladder. But best of all, it had a slide attached to it, so you could make a quick exit if a criminal climbed up into the tree house, or if your grandmother had already yelled for you five times that dinner was on the table.

Up in the tree house, Boone showed them how to look out the window through his special spyglass, which was really just the cardboard tube from a paper towel roll wrapped in silver duct tape. But if you squinted when you looked through it, it really did seem that you could see far, far away.

Boone also showed them his box of cryptozoologist tools. When he and Hugo grew up, they were going to be cryptozoologists. A cryptozoologist's job is to look for mysterious creatures. (This is how you say that word: CRIP-TOE-ZOE-OLOGIST. See, it's not that hard!) In the box, there was a flashlight, a compass, a journal, an old camera, and plaster of paris, so that if Boone found a footprint, he could make a mold of it.

Boone looked at Nogg. “Can I ask you a question?”

“Of course,” replied Nogg.

“What sort of creature are you?”

“What do you mean?” asked Nogg.

“I mean . . . what species are you?” Boone asked.

Hugo worried this might be rude, so under his breath he muttered to Boone, “Squatchicorn.”

“*What*-i-corn?” Boone asked.

Hugo cleared his throat. “Squatchicorn,” he muttered again.

But Nogg had overheard.

"What's a Squatchicorn?" Nogg asked.

Hugo looked at the confused expression on Nogg's face. "Um . . . not you, I'm guessing?"

"I'm a Sasquatch. Just like you," said Nogg.

"But Sasquatches can't grow horns," Hugo said.

"Neither can I," Nogg replied. Then he laughed. "Come on, I'll show you something."

12

The Golden Eye

They all slid down the tree house slide. It was the first time Hugo had ever been on a slide, so when he reached the bottom, he climbed back up to the tree house and slid down one more time.

Then Nogg led Boone and Hugo toward the banks of the river. For a few minutes,

Nogg walked back and forth, looking for something at the river's edge.

"Here we go!" he said. Crouching down, he dipped his hand into the shallow water and brought up a handful of mud. Then he went over to Boone.

"Take off your crown for a minute," Nogg told him.

Boone took the crown off, and Nogg plopped the mud right on Boone's head.

“Hey!” Boone protested.

“It’s just clay, Boone. Hold still.” Nogg worked the clay into a tuft of Boone’s hair, shaping and twisting until . . .

“Boone!” Hugo cried. “You have a horn on your head!”

Boone reached up to touch it, but Nogg warned, “Careful, you have to let the clay dry.”

"Wait. Is that how you got your horn, too?" Hugo asked, amazed.

Nogg nodded. "It's part of our clan's tradition. We call it the Golden Eye. You use your regular eyes to see the outside world," he explained. "But the Golden Eye helps you to know things that you *can't* see. Like when you get a hunch about something."

"Oh! Like when you have a hunch that your sister is going to flick you in the head, so you flick her first?" Hugo asked.

"Well . . . sort of," Nogg said.

"Does it really work?" Boone asked, gently touching the horn to see if the clay was drying.

"My father says that it works when you most need it to work," Nogg answered.

"Could you make a horn for me, too?" Hugo asked.

A few minutes later all three of them had horns on their foreheads. They looked at one another and smiled.

"Do you feel any different?" Hugo asked Boone.

Boone thought about it. "Not really," he said, "but when I stare at the tip of the horn, it helps me to cross my eyes better." He demonstrated, and Hugo had to admit he did it really well.

"So I guess you're just a regular type of Sasquatch, huh?" Boone said to Nogg. "When I first met you, I thought you were some kind of cryptid. Like Goatman or something."

"Or a Snallygaster," said Hugo, proud that he knew about Snallygasters.

"Or a Wheezing Mud Bat," said Nogg.

Hugo and Boone looked at him in surprise. "How do you know about Wheezing Mud Bats?" asked Hugo.

"Mad Marvin's Monster Cards, of

course," Nogg said, smiling. "I've got a whole box full of them."

"Did you have to leave the cards in Craggy Cavern?" Hugo asked.

Nogg nodded.

"That's awful!" Hugo cried. He himself had been collecting Mad Marvin's Monster Cards since he was a very little squidge. He couldn't imagine having to leave them behind.

"But that wasn't the worst thing," said Nogg. "The worst thing was that I left my notebook in my bedroom."

Hugo would rather have lost a dozen notebooks than even one of his Monster Cards.

“You can always get a new notebook,” Hugo said.

“This was a *special* notebook,” Nogg explained. “In order to become a Falcon Ranger Scout, I have to earn the North Woods Expert merit badge. Every time I hiked through the North Woods, I took that notebook and wrote down where all the streams and gullies and caverns and cliffs were. I’ve been doing that for a whole year and I was nearly finished . . .” Nogg shook his head. “Without the notebook, I’ll have to start all over again.”

“Where is Craggy Cavern?” Boone asked.

“Downriver a little ways,” Nogg replied.

"Then why can't you just go back there and get your notebook?" Boone asked.

So Nogg told him the story about the ghost. When he finished, Boone stood there for a moment, thinking.

"Let's go," Boone said decisively.

"Where?"

"To get your notebook. Come on, we can take my boat."

"We can't go back there," said Nogg. "It's too dangerous."

"There's a *ghost* in the cavern, Boone!" Hugo said. "A mean one."

Boone picked up his mangled crown and put it back on his head. "I hereby command us to get Nogg's notebook!"

There was nothing for Hugo and Nogg to do but follow the King's orders.

13

Craggy Cavern

Boone's little rowboat was bright red with the word *Voyajer* painted in white on its side. It was a sturdy boat, but two Sasquatches was a heavy load for her. When Hugo and Boone both sat in the back, the front reared up out of the water. In the end, Hugo sat in the back and Nogg sat in the front, with

Boone in the middle. That balanced things out nicely.

Hugo did the rowing. He loved to row, and his strong arms made the little boat zip through the water. The river wiggled this way and that, just like a Rippling Worm. Sometimes the riverbanks narrowed and the water rushed faster.

"Make her fly, Hugo!" Boone cried, and he put his hands in the air and whooped.

Nogg had never been on a boat before.

When they went fast, he held on to the sides at first, but after a while, he let go, put his hands in the air, and whooped along with Boone.

Sometimes there were rocky humps peeking out of the water where the riverbed was shallow, and Hugo had to go slowly and carefully around them.

After a while, the river grew wider and the thick woods crept closer to the banks.

"It's just up there," Nogg said, pointing to the right.

Hugo slowed his rowing and steered the *Voyajer* to the right. When they were close enough, Boone hopped into the shallow water and guided the boat to shore.

As they stood at the edge of the woods, Nogg sniffed the air and Hugo listened. No birds sang. The air was still.

"Wouldn't you rather make us do something more fun?" Hugo asked Boone.

"Nope," Boone said. He turned to Nogg and asked, "Which way?"

"This way," Nogg answered, and headed off into the woods.

Before long, they came to the mouth of Craggy Cavern. Boone reached into his back pocket, pulled out a flashlight, and handed it to Nogg.

"Stick close and stay quiet," Nogg warned.

Hugo was used to Widdershins Cavern, which was a busy and noisy place.

Sasquatches were always rushing here and there, shopping or visiting or going to school. Candle lanterns hung on the walls, always lit and giving everything a warm golden glow.

In Craggy Cavern, however, none of the lanterns were lit, so the passageways were full of dark shadows. As they walked, the only sounds they could hear were Boone's sneakers padding against the

ground, and occasionally a soft, cautious sniff from Nogg.

After walking down twisting passageways for several minutes, Hugo whispered nervously, "So where is the notebook?"

"In my bedroom, in the desk drawer," Nogg whispered back. "Our apartment is just a little farther ahead."

Out of the corner of his eye, Hugo spotted

something behind them. It was a small pale blue light, about the size of a walnut. It bobbed up and down in the dark, moving along the passageway as though it were following them.

"What is that?" Hugo cried as he spun around to look at it. But the light vanished in a wink.

"What did you see?" Nogg whispered.

"A light," Hugo said in a shaky voice. "The blue light."

Nogg shone the flashlight around, but the blue light was gone.

"We can turn back," Nogg suggested.

"No, we'll keep going," Boone commanded.

They continued on until finally Nogg

stopped in front of a rough wooden door.

"This is our apartment," Nogg said. He pushed the door open and led them down a hallway, past two rooms, and finally into his bedroom. Going directly to his desk, he opened the top drawer to get his notebook.

Hugo gazed all around, checking for the blue light and listening closely for the sound of knocking. Did the ghost know they were there? Hugo had an uneasy feeling that it did.

"That's weird!" Nogg said after a moment.

"What is?" asked Hugo.

"The notebook's gone."

"Are you sure?" Boone asked.

Nogg shone the flashlight in the drawer again. "Positive. It's not here."

Just then, Hugo saw the blue light appear again, hovering near the entrance to Nogg's room, close to the ground.

"*Pssst*," Hugo hissed to the others, then

pointed at the light. For a moment, they all stared at it as it hung in the air, bobbing slightly in the darkness.

"It's watching us," Nogg whispered.

Hugo felt a prickly feeling on his forehead, right on the spot where the Golden Eye was. It might have just been because the clay was drying. Or it might have just been that he had an itch on his forehead.

But Hugo didn't think so. Because suddenly he had a hunch.

The blue light darted away, out of the apartment.

"Let's go!" Hugo cried.

"Where?" Boone called.

"To wherever the light is going!" Hugo called back.

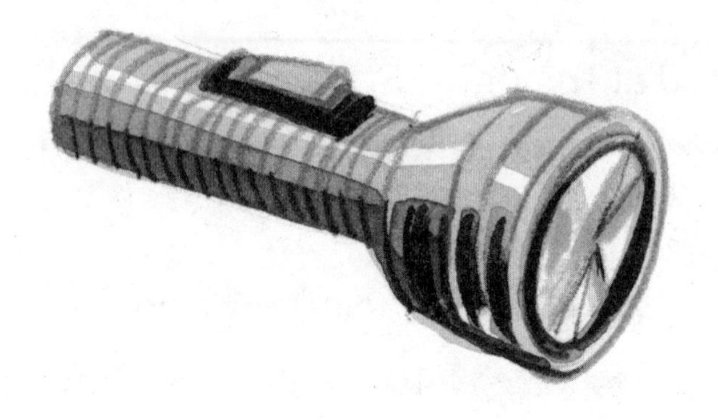

14

The Blue Light

They chased the blue light as it flew down one passageway and turned down another and then another, staying far ahead of them. All at once it veered left, then disappeared through a doorway.

"It's going into our school," Nogg said.

A moment later, they stood at the

school's doorway. The blue light had disappeared again.

"This is my classroom," Nogg told them, shining the flashlight around the room. There were no posters on the walls or reading lofts, just desks. Hugo thought it wasn't nearly as nice as his school in Widdershins Cavern.

"See that?" Nogg aimed the flashlight at the back of the classroom. There were rocks all over the floor, some of them very large. "That's where the wall caved in after we heard the knocking." He pointed the flashlight at a desk that was smashed to bits. "That was my desk."

"Holy cats," Boone said quietly.

Out of the corner of his eye, Hugo

spotted the blue light in the next room, darting about wildly.

"There it is!" he cried. They dashed into the other classroom, but by the time they got there, the blue light had disappeared once more.

"And *poof*, it's gone," said Boone.

"This is Yama's classroom," Nogg said, pointing the flashlight at the small desks. The cavern's walls were lined with shelves full of paint and brushes and pots of glue. On a table in the corner was a display of miniature houses.

Hugo felt that prickly feeling in his Golden Eye again.

"What are these?" Hugo asked as he walked up to the little houses.

“Fairy houses,” Nogg told him. “The younger squidges made them.”

They were built out of bark and moss and clay. Some of them were lopsided and some of them were nothing more than twigs leaning up against one another. But there was one that was very well made and

as big as a dollhouse. It had windows with curtains and a little door painted blue. The roof was made of pinecone scales and it had its own chimney that was covered in moss.

"That's Yama's fairy house," Nogg said when he saw Hugo looking at it.

Carefully, Hugo wiggled the roof on Yama's fairy house. It was glued down, but with a few more wiggles, he was able to lift it off the house and look inside.

"Whoa!" he exclaimed.

"What?" Nogg rushed over and aimed the flashlight directly into Yama's fairy house.

Piled in the house were all sorts of things—candles, a river-stone bracelet, a

small fox carved out of wood, a whittling knife, a toy lantern, a wooden spoon, a doll in a green cap lying down on a tiny bed with a handkerchief blanket, a piece of honey-drop candy, and dozens of other things.

Nogg reached into the house and pulled out a blue sash covered with colorful wooden badges pinned to it.

"My merit badges," he said, shaking his head in bewilderment. He put the sash around his neck, then sifted through the pile of things in the fairy house. "There's Mrs. Wikpik's bracelet and that's my dad's knife, and there's my cousin's slingshot . . ." He stopped and sighed. "No notebook, though."

"Sorry, Nogg," Boone said.

"I guess it must have been Yama who was stealing things," Nogg said sadly. "I just don't understand. It's not like her . . ."

It was then that Hugo reached into the fairy house, and with the tip of his finger, he knocked the green hat off the little doll's head. In a flash, the doll leapt out of the bed, bit Hugo's finger, and snatched his hat from off the fairy house floor.

15

The Thief

They all watched in amazement as the little man put his hat back on and adjusted the small hammer that was tucked in his belt. He was no taller than a squirrel when it sits up on its haunches to eat a nut.

"He's *real*," whispered Nogg.

"He's a Tommyknocker," both Hugo

and Boone said at the same time.

Boone looked at Hugo in surprise.

"How did you know that?" Boone asked Hugo. Boone was usually the one who knew all about cryptids.

"I read about them in your book," Hugo told him. "See that little lantern?" He pointed to the small brass lantern by the Tommyknocker's feet. "I think that was the blue light."

"Then you knew the blue light wasn't really a ghost?" Boone asked him.

"I didn't *know* know," Hugo replied. "But I had a hunch."

"What *is* a Tommyknocker?" Nogg asked.

"They're little creatures who live in mines and caves," Hugo told him. "They like to steal things." The Tommyknocker made a huffy sound, as though he found this insulting.

"Hey, wait a second," Nogg said suspiciously. He reached into the fairy house and yanked the handkerchief off the Tommyknocker's bed. Underneath was a little black notebook.

"He was using my notebook for a mattress!" Nogg said, snatching it out of the house. He glowered at the Tommyknocker. "Little thief!"

In response, the Tommyknocker picked up the honey-drop candy and chucked it at Nogg's head.

"I wouldn't be too mad at him," said Hugo. "He was trying to help you."

"How? By stealing our stuff?"

"No, by knocking. Many years ago, Humans who worked in mine shafts always wanted to have a Tommyknocker with them, even though Tommyknockers

stole things. That's because mining is dangerous work. Roofs can collapse, rocks can fall on you. But right before something dangerous happened, Tommyknockers would bang on the walls with their hammers to warn the miners."

"So that knocking we heard before the rocks fell was the Tommyknocker?" Nogg asked. "He was warning us?"

Hugo nodded. "And from the looks of

your desk, I think he might have saved your life."

Nogg stared at the Tommyknocker. The little man was standing in front of the pile of stolen items with his arms crossed over

his chest, as if daring them to take back any more things.

"I'd like to thank him," said Nogg. "Do Tommyknockers talk?"

Boone bent over the fairy house and said to the Tommyknocker in a loud voice, "DO YOU TALK?"

In response, the Tommyknocker picked up the wooden spoon and launched it at Boone, who dodged away just in time.

"Hard to tell," Boone said.

Nogg unpinned one of the wooden badges from his sash and held it up.

"This is a Ranger Scout merit badge," Nogg told the Tommyknocker. "This badge is really hard to earn. It's for Acts of Heroism." Nogg carefully placed the little badge on the Tommyknocker's pile of things.

The Tommyknocker stared up at Nogg. Beneath the bushy brows, his eyes were sharp and bright. Then, as if he understood, he removed his hat and bowed.

16

Birthday Wish

It was a very happy boat ride home. They had faced danger and darkness and a possible ghost, yet things had turned out fine in the end, which always puts everyone in a good mood.

They were traveling upstream now, so the *Voyajer* was moving at a leisurely pace as Hugo rowed. Nogg had his notebook

open and was jotting down notes. Boone was gazing up at the wispy clouds and smiling.

"You know something?" Boone said. "This is the best birthday I've ever had."

"But I ate your cake," Hugo said. He had nearly forgotten about that little disaster, and now that he was reminded, he felt bad all over again.

"It doesn't matter, because I still got to make my birthday wish. And guess what? The wish actually came true."

"It did? What did you wish for?" Hugo asked.

"I wished for an adventure that we could include in our book," said Boone. To Nogg he explained, "One day I'm going to write a book about my adventures with Hugo. It's going to be called *The Adventures of Big Foot and Little Foot*. Now I can include a chapter about Tommyknockers."

"That's true!" Hugo said, already feeling better.

"Anyway," Boone added, "I bet my grandma is baking us a new birthday cake right now." He tapped his Golden Eye. "Just a hunch."

And you know what? He was right!

17
The North Woods

On Sunday morning, Hugo was in the kitchen of the Everything-You-Need General Store and Bakery. He was helping Grandpa make raspberry snarfles, which are a lot like waffles, except they are shaped like oak leaves. Grandpa was mixing the batter, and Hugo was working the snarfle iron.

Hugo still had his Golden Eye on his forehead, but the very end of it was bent upward.

"Looks like your horn ran into some trouble," Grandpa said.

"Yeah, and the trouble's name is Winnie," Hugo said dryly. "She found out that I was the one who took all the straw out of her pillow, so she bent my horn."

Grandpa laughed. "So what did you think of the Human house?" he asked Hugo.

Hugo considered for a moment. "Well, everything was very smooth and bright. And they have interesting spoons. It was nice, I guess. But I like my own home better." He opened up the snarfle iron and stacked the steaming snarfles on a plate. "Grandpa, do you think we might have to leave Widdershins Cavern one day?"

"I suppose it could happen."

"I would hate it."

"So would I," Grandpa said. "But no matter where we live, we'll have our family and our friends with us. That's all that counts, when you come right down to it."

"But what if we have to move far away from Boone?" Hugo asked.

"Good friends have a way of finding each other again."

Hugo supposed so. But still, he hoped that he and Boone would always live exactly where they lived now, forever and ever.

The kitchen door swung open and Nogg walked in, holding a very large box in his arms.

“I just came to say goodbye,” Nogg told them.

“You’re leaving already?!” Hugo cried. He had hoped they would stay at Widdershins Cavern for at least a few days longer.

“We’re heading to the east end of Ripple

Worm River to look for a new home," Nogg said.

"Then you're not going back to Craggy Cavern?"

"No. Even though the clan knows that the ghost was really a Tommyknocker, they think that the cave-ins make it too dangerous."

There was a dull thump from inside the box.

"In a minute!" Nogg said to the box. Then to Hugo and Grandpa he explained, "Some of us went to Craggy Cavern early this morning to pack up a few things."

Nogg put the box on the counter, and Hugo and Grandpa peered inside to see Yama's fairy house. Nogg lifted off the

house's roof. The Tommyknocker was standing inside, glaring up at them with a cranky look on his face. When he spotted

Hugo, he hissed and grabbed onto his green cap, just in case Hugo decided to knock it off his head again.

"You're taking the Tommyknocker with you?" Hugo asked, surprised.

"It seemed a shame to leave him there all by himself," Nogg replied. "Yama plans to build him a swimming pool." The Tommyknocker made a little whistle of satisfaction at this. Then he put his hands on his hips and stamped his feet a few times.

"All *right*! We're going!" Nogg told him. Then Nogg reached into the box and pulled out a piece of rolled-up paper.

"This is for you and Boone," he said, handing it to Hugo. "It's a map of the North

Woods. I used the notes in my notebook to draw it."

"Thank you!" Hugo said, taking the map.

"I figured you could include it in your book," Nogg said. "You know, *The Adventures of Big Foot and Little Foot*. That way, everyone could see where all your adventures happened."

There was another impatient stomp from inside the fairy house.

"I'd better get going," Nogg said, picking up the box. "I'll write you a letter when we have a new home."

After he left, Hugo unrolled the map and laid it flat on the kitchen counter. It was a beautiful map, and he and Grandpa marveled at all the details.

CRAGGY CAVERN
SLIPPERY SLOPE
LOG
RASPBERRY BUSH
BURROW
RIPPLE WORM RIVER
MEADOW
FIVE HEMLOCKS
GIANT OAK
MUD POOL
BLUEBERRY BUSH
WIDDERSHINS CAVERN
SUNNY MOUNTAINS
FARMS ←
North

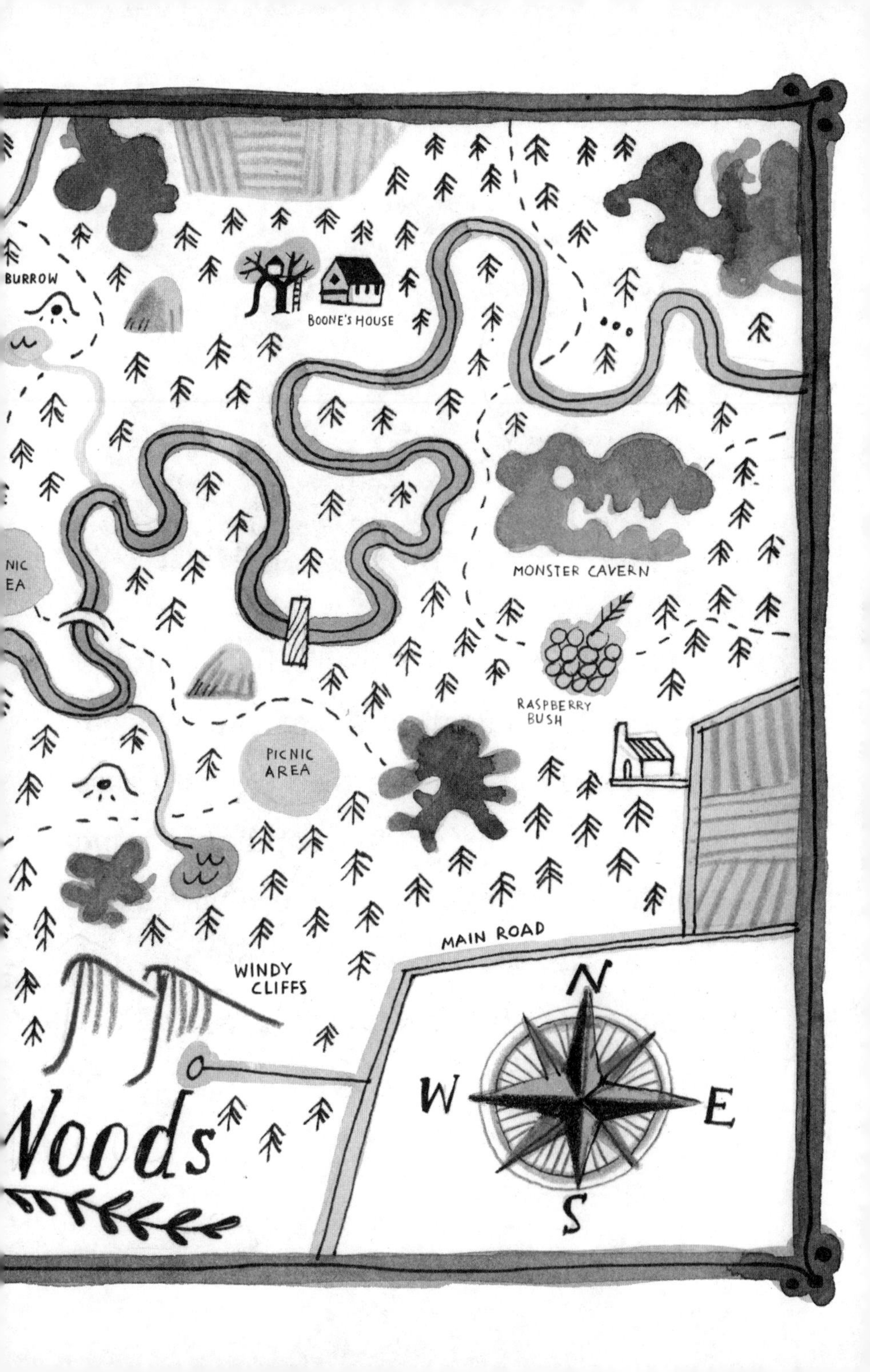
BURROW
BOONE'S HOUSE
NIC
EA
MONSTER CAVERN
RASPBERRY
BUSH
PICNIC
AREA
MAIN ROAD
WINDY
CLIFFS
Noods
N
W
E
S

"There's Boone's house!" Hugo pointed to the little house that Nogg had labeled. He'd even included the tree house. Hugo placed his finger on the winding Ripple Worm River. "And that's where we rowed the *Voyajer* all the way to"—he slid his finger along the twists and turns of the river, then stopped to tap on a drawing of a cavern—"Craggy Cavern!"

It was all there and so much more. The map showed the Sasquatch footpaths and the raspberry and blueberry bush patches. It showed the best spots for picnics and for finding mushrooms. Nogg had marked all the steep slopes that were good for sledding in the winter and rolling downhill in the summer, and there were dozens of mysterious-looking caves and burrows and cliffs. The North Woods stretched out farther in every direction than Hugo had ever imagined.

"There's an awful lot of Big Wide World out there," Grandpa murmured dreamily.

"And anything can happen in it," Hugo said, smiling.

ACKNOWLEDGMENTS

Sasquatches know that we all need help if we want to do things right, and that's why I want to thank my wonderful "Sasquatch Community." Major thanks to my editor, Erica Finkel, for her clear-sighted wisdom. I am forever grateful to my agent, Alice Tasman, who is even better than thirty jars of acorn butter. Thanks to Felicita Sala for bringing Hugo and his friends to life with her beautiful illustrations. Big thanks to my publicist, Kimberley Moran, and the entire Abrams team for spreading the word about Hugo and Boone. And finally, as always, thanks to my practically perfect husband, Adam, and my own squidge, Ian.

ELLEN POTTER is the award-winning author of many books for children, including the Olivia Kidney series, *Slob*, *The Kneebone Boy*, and most recently, the Piper Green and the Fairy Tree series. She lives in Maine.

FELICITA SALA is the self-taught illustrator of many books for children. She lives with her husband and daughter in Rome, Italy.

CHECK OUT THE WHOLE SERIES!

BIG FOOT
and LITTLE FOOT
THE MONSTER DETECTOR
Story by Ellen Potter
Art by Felicita Sala

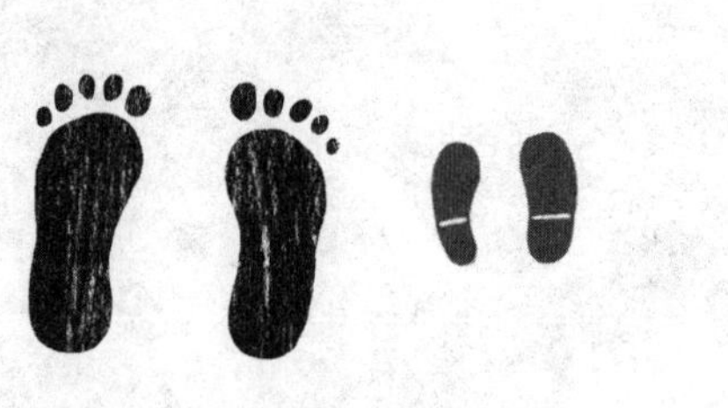